The Plankton Collector

The Plankton Collector

Cath Barton

New Welsh Rarebyte is the book imprint of New Welsh Review Ltd,
PO Box 170, Aberystwyth, Wales, SY23 1WZ,
www.newwelshreview.com, @newwelshreview,
Facebook.com/newelshreview
© Cath Barton, 2018
ISBN 978-1-9161501-2-6

Editor: Gwen Davies
Design & typesetting: Ingleby Davies Design
Cover image: Bozena Fulawka/Shutterstock.com
Printed in Europe by Pulsio

New Welsh Review Ltd works with the financial support of the
Welsh Books Council & Aberystwyth University

For my mum (1921–2014), without whom....

In the Beginning

Take a sea shore, let us say one on the leeward coast of an island, where the twice-daily coming-in and going-out of the sea is, in the main, a calming. There are cliffs of old rock, gneisses and schists, born of a time of greater drama. On the tops is a green sward, pockmarked by holes where rabbits burrow. They emerge at dawn and dusk and nibble the grass back into tidiness. On the cliffs is a congregation of gannets, kittiwakes and puffins. They sing songs from the hymnal of the birds. They are raucous and out of time with one another. On the shoreline a few of them land and strut about, self-important but awkward because they are out of their element.

Here the morning light is pearlescent. There is a shimmer to it. Water laps gently around rocks tumbled long ago on the shore, making the little curtains of green algae move back and forth as if they were opening and closing on the scenes of a play. Which indeed they are. It is the daily play of the creatures of the rocky shore, the sand-bubbler crabs which emerge from their sandy nests and scuttle in sideways motion, the cushion stars which scavenge on them after death and the pink polyps of hydroids which feed on plankton. Much of this, and especially the plankton, is invisible to the man we see who passes by and remarks on his disappointment that the rocky pools are not as they were in his childhood. He is thinking about those long-ago summers of (we remember erroneously) unremitting sunshine when boys wearing long shorts or short longs lifted strands of jellified seaweeds aloft triumphantly, for mother to take a picture with the Box Brownie. That picture which will be amongst the snaps which she keeps all her life in the old chocolate box, the captured iconic moments of seaside holidays, made happy by a trick of memory.

And now, and now, the rock pools are in fact no different. Their evolution is on a different scale to that of humankind. The passage from boyhood to manhood is but a passing breeze upon the waves of the oceans, where even those rare people who can hold their breath for minutes and can dive deep are prey to sudden cold currents, which will suck that breath from them and carry it away for ever. Away to places where the sounds of the depths will be their funeral oration, but where the largest of the whales still depend upon those tiny plankton for continued life, as do we all.

The diatoms of the kingdom Protista, which live in microscopic glass boxes wandering the oceans, release enough oxygen to give all of us now on Earth our every fifth breath. And when they die their tiny coffins sink to the sea bed. We see them as tiny shells. Some of them lie now in the rock pools of this shore, and it is here that the Plankton Collector will come, with his net of the closest mesh, and gather them. He is a man like any other, who played in rock pools in his childhood, just as other visitors to this shoreline did.

No-one knows his name, or rather they know him by different names, depending on when and where they meet him. All he asks is to to be acknowledged and listened to but, like the plankton, he is a wanderer – though on land rather than in water – and is never in one place for long. He passes unremarked in the crowd. He is the man at the next table in the café. The one drinking his morning coffee like any other. The one reading the newspaper. Or the one simply sitting and staring.

He has been doing his work for many years unrecognised by most of us. He goes to those who are ready and willing to receive his help.

1

Summer

Look. We are approaching a country house, somewhere in the middle of England. It is high summer. On either side of the road are fields of wheat, divided by small copses of trees. It is before the time of the terrible tree diseases. There is oak, ash and, standing proud on the roadsides, soaring elm. The harvesters are out, the blades clanking, the dust rising as the grain is separated and poured into a hopper. The noise is, though, faint by the time it reaches the garden of the house. It is reduced to a background noise which sings in counterpoint to the humming of the bees on the lavenders which border the path on the western side of the lawn. Hoops are positioned on the lawn for a croquet match which will take place tomorrow, or the day after, or one day in the future. It is, as we approach, a little after four in the afternoon. Shadows are beginning to spread their fingers across the lawn. The family of the house are taking tea, not together around a white-clothed table as you might imagine, but each one in a separate world. Father sits with a straight back in a wicker chair on the veranda on the south-eastern side of the house. Here he feels the warmth of the afternoon sun but is sheltered from its direct impact by the stand of pine trees beyond the southern corner of the croquet lawn. He appears to be reading a book, but look, he is not turning the pages and his head nods forward and then snaps sharply back as he hears footfall. It is Mother approaching with a tea tray. We are too far away to hear what one says to the other, but we can see that it is a brief, routine exchange, tinged, if we could but feel it, with an ineffable sadness.

Mother turns and calls across the garden. If we cannot make out the words we can nonetheless sense the intention, which is to call her children. And look, here they come, two boys on the cusp of adolescence. The elder, Edgar, is gangly and ginger-headed like his mother; the other, Bunny, short and, taking after his father, dark-haired. As they run across the lawn the taller one catches his foot in a croquet hoop and stumbles, but he does not lose his balance and catches up with his brother to grab at sandwiches, cakes and glasses of squash and sit down on the steps leading up to the veranda to munch and drink.

Mother shields her eyes against the sun which, at the place

where she stands, will otherwise dazzle her. She is scanning the horizon, but she cannot see her third child, a girl, who is sitting in the orchard, lost in a book. Mother knows that the girl, her youngest, is there and in a minute, look, she is walking down to the orchard with a tray of tea things. She spoils this child, for she sees in her the girl she had once been herself, full of innocent potential. The girl is grateful, but she does not show it, and Mother's step is a little heavier with disappointment as she returns along the gravel path to the house and its kitchen, where she will stop for a few minutes, perch on a stool, drink a cup of tea and eat a sandwich and just a small slice of cake.

This is an afternoon like many others for the family. But look, already the leaves of the corkscrew willow are yellowing, presaging the decays of autumn and the deep sleeps of winter.

Autumn

Just two months have passed and look at the change. Or rather, look and see who is there at the house and who is not. The autumn is warm and Mother is weeding and tidying in the garden, but she is distracted, moving from task to task, settling at none. There is no sign of Father. It is a Sunday, he should surely be at home. The garage doors are closed, but if we could open them and look inside we would see that the car is not there. Mother is constantly pausing in her work, and stands to stretch her back, looking each time towards the house, her eyes raised to a window at the extreme western end of the second floor. There is anxiety etched in lines on her face and the veins stand out on her neck. If we could but perceive it we would see that her whole body is taut with tension, with the worry that has been building up over the past weeks. She narrows her eyes and pushes her chin out, as if straining to hear something from the room on the second floor. Then maybe she does, for she drops her clippings and rushes in. Soon after that the younger boy and his sister appear at the kitchen door, hanging back as if they are being pushed out. Then, taking the plunge, they dart off in opposite directions.

Mary – that is the girl's name – can be no older than ten. She wears a frock of buttercup yellow with scalloped pockets. There is a swing in the orchard. Look over there now – the flashes of yellow show she is swinging higher and higher. If we had sharp ears we would hear the chains holding the slatted wooden seat creaking, and intermittent small thumps as Mary jumps from the highest point of the swing's trajectory, daring herself to do so over and over until, in a while, she returns towards the house and we can see a tear in one of the pockets of the yellow frock. She walks slowly, scuffing her shoes on the gravel of the path, reluctant perhaps to face her mother, who made the frock, which is meant to be kept for best. And the more so because her mother has, as she told Mary when she sent her and her brother out to play, already enough to worry about.

As night falls, lights come on in the house. There is a light in the kitchen, where Mary is reading an adventure story, something into which she can escape, escape from what she cannot explain or even describe, but feels as a dragging pain in her heart. There are lights in two rooms on the second floor of the house. One of them is Bunny's bedroom. He escapes by burrowing into his bed. The other is where Mother sits with Edgar, because Edgar is sick and, for him, bed is not an escape but a prison. And there is no room in which we can see Father, for he is still not home.

Winter

Look now at the house in winter. Look into Bunny's bedroom window. He has woken as suddenly and completely as if someone had turned on a light. Though there is, as yet, no light. He sits, throws his legs off the bed, snuggles his toes into his slippers and pulls a blanket round his shoulders before padding to the window. He peeks between the curtains. Over to the left he can just make out the bulk of the church and the shapes of the gravestones below, dark on dark. He shivers as he remembers Magwitch rising up in the film they'd watched at school. It had made him afraid of their graveyard, that film. There was a time when he and Edgar used to play there, but now he would not go, for fear of what might happen.

Then, listen, the noise which must have woken him comes again out of the dark. A low sobbing from the far end of the corridor. Now his mother's quick step on the bare floorboards of the back staircase. Bunny can bear to hear no more. He scuttles back and into bed without taking off his slippers, and burrows down, down and away from it all.

When he wakes again there is a grey light coming through

the curtains and his mother is calling to him to get up. Down in the kitchen she ladles out porridge for the boy and his sister and tells them that they should go out and get some fresh air.

'It's the shortest day, it'll be over before you know, you should make the most of it,' she says, frowning and pulling on her coat. She hesitates, then blurts out, 'I have to fetch the doctor. Edgar is worse.'

'Is he going to die?' asks Mary.

Mother turns away to hide the tears which spring at the brutal question, and Mary jumps up from the table and dashes from the room. Bunny spoons in the hateful, solid porridge and says nothing. A slam of the kitchen door and Mother is gone. No sound from upstairs. Bunny wants to go and see Edgar. There is something he wanted to ask him about Magwitch. But he is scared, because of the sickness. He scratches at the breadcrumbs in the cracks of the table with the handle of his spoon. Abruptly, without deciding to do it, he gets up and goes to the door that leads to the back stairs. He opens it. The house creaks.

Bunny sets off up the stairs, but a sudden whimpering makes him freeze. Were we closer we would hear the whimpering turn to loud sobs. The boy retreats into the safety of the warm kitchen, closing the door against his brother's cries. He pulls on his coat and galoshes, goes out of the kitchen door and, leaving the garden by the side gate, stomps off across the winter mud.

The hedges are full of small birds foraging for seeds. Bunny stands and watches them, hands clenching and unclenching in his pockets. He looks back at the house. It sits like a weight upon the land, the sky behind it empty. Bunny gazes at the birds and wishes that he could flit and fly like them. He trudges across to the churchyard wall, skirting round the copse where he and Edgar had once found a dying fox. There are shiny black beetles on some fresh dung and he pokes at them with a stick, turning them over and casting them aside. Their legs flail. Bunny brings the stick down with a thump, thump, thump. It makes him feel better.

But the light is failing, he has to get home. The mud sucks at his boots as he walks, slowing him down. By the time he reaches the kitchen door it is quite dark. He realises he is very hungry, finds the heel of the loaf and stuffs it into his mouth, fast. Too fast because there are sounds coming from upstairs, then feet on the staircase and his mother's face, red and blotchy, the doctor's behind, long and solemn. Bunny pushes past them and up to his room, trailing crumbs and hot tears.

Look now for a moment at Mary in her bedroom, lost in her book. She hears the commotion, but as if it is very far away, as if it is something happening to another family.

By the time Father comes home it is all over. Look, he wants to comfort his wife, but he cannot. He does not know how, and he is ashamed.

2

I'm ten years and four months old. I have two older brothers, Edgar and Bunny. Edgar got sick though and he died. It was two days before my birthday, and I didn't have a cake. I think Mother forgot, but I didn't dare say.

I always play on my own. I don't mind that, not really. At school I have friends, but if they come to the house once they never return. On summer days I used to sit on my own in the orchard and read. Mother would bring me milk and a plate of sandwiches at teatime and tell me to remember what a lucky girl I was. I doubt if that will happen next summer though.

Watch me now. I'm running along a path in the woods and the shadows from the trees are making a shifting pattern of circles on the ground. I brush against something that stings but I don't stop, I mustn't stop. I have to get away from the house because Mother is always crying.

Now then look, look, you'll see the man. I saw his feet first and stopped just in time. I tried to dodge round him but I couldn't.

Mary, Mary quite contrary
How does your garden grow?
With silver bells and cockle shells
And pretty maids all in a row.

He sang that song to me. That was when I knew I would go with him, although I didn't even know his name then. But he knew mine, and that mattered to me more than anything. I was used to not being noticed, not being listened to. He said he was going to show me something important, if I chose to travel with him. I went with him because I knew it was the right thing for me to do and that I would be safe with him. I knew that in a place deep inside.

***

The day that Mary met the Plankton Collector was a day like any other. For many people, all days are like any other when they start. You open your eyes onto a world with which you are completely familiar. You have a routine and you follow it. You may or may not consider yourself happy, but your routine is in some way a comfort to you. It measures out your days, morning, afternoon, evening and then it is time for bed, to enter the mystery of restoring sleep. We may say to one another, over our morning coffee, the first pause of the day, that we are bored, want an adventure of some kind, but if and when something or someone comes along to throw our routine in the air we are not content with the disordered way in which the pieces come down. We crave the old routine. What we know suits us, imperfect as it is.

Mary, being just ten years and (she will insist on this) four months old, is not yet fixed in a routine. Yes, she goes to school each day from Monday to Friday, and she does what homework her teachers require of her. But generally in the evenings and at weekends she can do whatever she wishes. She does not have the busy schedule which will, by the time she is an old woman, have shackled the children who are growing up then. Mary is free to drift and to dream, which is exactly what she does. She spends a lot of time in the garden, the orchard, the woods.

And so it was, that on a day like any other – but we might note that, after the longest of winters, the first daffodils had finally appeared in the grass of the orchard – Mary met a man like any other. Except that he is not really like any other and the day is one which Mary will always remember. She had, of course, been told by her parents never to speak to strange men. She was an obedient child and furthermore she knew – even in those days children knew – what could happen. But she trusted this man and said she would go with him. She knew that her mother would worry when she did not return for tea, but she knew also that in the long run this journey would be more important and that, ultimately, her mother would understand. She did not say as much in as many words to herself, but, later, she would tell people that she did know, inside.

This man is a little like the Pied Piper of Hamelin, or Svengali, or Dr Who, and yet he is like none of these. He sings, but he does not hypnotise, neither does he offer time travel, at least not to other galaxies. Inside our own world he is certainly a traveller. Think of this: when you last walked through the centre of your town, you might well have passed him. The connection is like one of which we all have experience: someone asks you to put up a visiting friend of theirs for the night, a stranger to you, and you find that you have a good friend in common, one who lives somewhere else entirely. You laugh about that together. It is not something to be frightened about. Neither is it if you meet this man. It is time we gave him a name, so on this occasion let us call him Mr Smith.

Mr Smith suggested to Mary, on that spring day, that the two of them should take a train journey together, the railway being close by and the trains, in those days before Dr Beeching initiated their decline, quite frequent. They took the Down train, simply because it came first. They got into a compartment which was already occupied by a young boy travelling with an older woman, who they took to be his grandmother. The boy looked at Mary's travelling companion with suspicion, but when Mr Smith produced a little ginger kitten the boy and Mary were both entranced, and played with the creature for the whole of the journey. Mr Smith said the kitten was called Charlie, and Mary felt something like a feather tickling her neck. She started to say, 'That was my brother's,' but thought better of it. What she was going to say was that it was her brother Edgar's middle name, but she didn't want anyone asking about Edgar.

They all got off the train at a little town called something by-the-Sea, or on-Sea or next-the-Sea. Afterwards Mary couldn't remember the name, just that it was, indeed, by the sea. She and the boy ran along the beach and built sandcastles and decorated them with tiny shells, while their travelling companions sat on an upturned boat and chatted.

Only later, when they were sitting in a hotel dining room supping brown soup, just the two of them, did Mary remember Charlie the kitten and she asked Mr Smith what had happened to him.

'He'll be fine,' he said, as if he was talking about a grown person, not a defenceless kitten.

Mary felt horrified. 'But,' she began.

'Don't worry,' Mr Smith continued. 'Trust me, he'll be fine. I just asked him along to remind you of your brother.'

Mary gulped. She felt, quite suddenly, so tired that she thought she might lay her head down in the soup bowl then and there, like the dormouse getting into the tea pot at the Mad Hatter's tea party. She put down her soup spoon, dabbed her mouth with the big white starched napkin and asked, very quietly, if she might go to her bed now, please. Mr Smith did not argue. The girl found her way up the wide winding staircase and next thing she knew, her mother was tucking her up in bed at home. Mary lay awake for a while, though, wondering. Had it all been a daydream? Why had

Mother not been cross with her? It made no sense.

Her mother sat by Mary's bedside for a little. The darkening room and her daughter's gentle breathing helped to calm her. Her husband was still up in town, whatever 'in town' meant. She did not want to entertain her suspicions. She wanted to reach out and stroke Mary's hair, but she feared waking her. If only her husband would walk through the door and bend with a kiss to her neck. Or was it another from whom she really desired this? Again she dared not entertain the thought. Instead she concentrated on this little oasis, the counterpane which rose and fell infinitesimally with the little girl's breathing, two or three brief bright flashes of light from the last of the sun's rays through the half-closed curtains, the small sound of a mouse in the wall cavity.

She reached down for the yellow frock which Mary had dropped carelessly on the floor and pressed out its creases over her knee. She needed to mend the tear in one of the pockets. It had been there for too long. As she shook the dress and folded it over her arm, some tiny shells tumbled out of the torn pocket and dropped with small noises onto the bare floorboards. It was as if they sounded from the bed of a deep ocean. She froze and held her breath as Mary stirred, opened and closed her mouth but did not wake. Then she bent down, carefully gathered as many of the shells as she could and walked on tip-toe out of the room, closing the door behind her with a gentle click of the latch.

Once downstairs the girl's mother went into the sitting room and turned on a lamp on a small table by the wing armchair. It was the place she always took her sewing. She placed the yellow frock over the arm of the chair and dropped the shells onto the table, where they glistened. They were more like glass than shell, seen in the light of the lamp, but had a definite scent of the sea. How and where had Mary got them, she wondered. She sat, picked up her needle-case and threaded a needle with buttercup-yellow cotton. The sudden noise of the sitting room door opening made her start and the needle pierced the skin of her right index-finger, drawing blood. She raised her finger to her mouth, sucking at the spurt of red before it had time to drop and stain the frock. Which was how her husband saw her as he entered the room. He had been determined to speak his truth to his wife that evening, but his resolution drained away as he saw her sitting there in the penumbra of the lamp. She was still much too fragile, he realised. And so he merely mumbled an apology for the lateness of his train and she nodded, complicit in the lie.

Upstairs Mary was awake and had heard the comforting sound of the door which signalled her father's arrival home. As soon as her mother had gone Mary had opened her eyes and stayed with them open in the darkness for a long time. The little shells tinkling on the floor had awoken her after all and she had known immediately what the sound was, known also in that moment that she really had gone on a journey with the man called Mr Smith. She went over it all in her mind time and again, Charlie the kitten on the train and the sand-castle which she and the boy had made and decorated with those shells. She needed to fix the details in her mind so that she could go to that place when things got too difficult at home.

One by one, the four occupants of the house fell asleep in their separate beds, Mother, Father and their two children. Downstairs, the Plankton Collector came to retrieve the tiny shells which the woman had picked up and which she would for now forget, but he left those few which remained on Mary's bedroom floor so that the child would remember their journey together.

3

I was happiest before I was married, when people called me by my name rather than Mother. In those post-war days I lived in an attic flat in West Hampstead with my friend Sally. I took the bus to work down Kilburn High Road and even when the raindrops streaming down the windows blurred the windows of the shops I sometimes felt I would burst with happiness. The office was a quiet and comfortable haven. I worked all morning at the figures, adding, rubbing out, and drawing a bottom line by lunchtime, if all was going well, with a settling satisfaction. On winter days Sally and I would meet in the Kardomah, then when the spring opened up we'd go to Regent's Park and crumble the crusts of our spam sandwiches for the birds.

Once a month on a Saturday night we dressed up and went to the Lyceum, to the dance, and sat with our legs neatly tucked under our chairs waiting. I wouldn't say one of us was luckier than the other, we both got plenty of invitations. But the best part of the evening was when we got out from the fug of the dance. Sometimes we missed the last bus, but we felt so giddy the walk home was almost like floating above the pavement, till we clattered through the door and our landlady sounded out about the noise at that time of night and we just giggled all the way up the stairs and got into our night clothes and Sally would sit on the end of my bed or I on hers and we'd talk and laugh and laugh about which man had danced best and which had tried to be fresh, till sleep got the better of us both.

Our dreams, waking and sleeping, were of the handsome stranger who would appear one Saturday, and we swore eternal friendship and how we would be one another's bridesmaids. I would choose buttercup yellow for her dress, I said, it would suit her complexion so well.

And then there was the accident. Sally shouldn't have been there, on her way to the office. It should have been her day off, and I blamed myself for not stopping her, but how could I have, that's what everyone said and of course they were right, there was no way I could have stopped her going, she was always one to be helpful, and neither of us, no-one could have known that that car driver would have a heart attack, it happens, every day it happens, but why did it have to be Sally who was crossing the road just at that moment?

And then it was just me in the attic flat, and my days at work were all grey and I didn't go to the Lyceum on Saturdays any more, because I felt so sad and lonely and that no man would want to dance with me, so why ask for disappointment. But one spring day in the park David sat by me, he was so polite how could I refuse him the space, and he said perhaps he would see me there again and I was powerless to say no. Or to say no when, six months later, after several cups of tea together in the Kardomah, he asked me to go to the pictures with him and then things spooled out as if I was in the film myself rather than simply watching it. In the wedding pictures David is smiling and so am I, and of course I couldn't tell him that my heart was aching because I had no bridesmaid in buttercup yellow organza, just my sister in a suit of dusty blue which she had insisted on and I had never been able to argue with my sister. I would have wished her dead instead of Sally, but I could never have told anyone that, certainly not David. His own sister had died young, he had told me, and his eyes glistened when he spoke of her. Which I understood, of course I did, but when on the first night of our honeymoon he spoke more of his late lamented sister than of me, I began to shrink from him.

I have, nonetheless, been a good wife to David. I put his meals on the table and I have given him children. Three beautiful children. But we have lost Edgar and now I am adrift.

***

The spring, being late, came that year with an abundance of colour and scent on which everyone remarked. Each day from Monday to Friday David travelled up to town, Bunny and Mary went to school and their mother Rose busied herself in the garden and, in the afternoon before the children got home, walked over to the churchyard and spent time at Edgar's grave. It was there, one Thursday in early May, that she met the Plankton Collector. She took him at first for another mourner, for he spent some time apparently tending a new grave. Unwilling to impose upon another's grief or, more likely, aggravate her own, Rose kept her head down, concentrating on her book. She liked to read poetry in the graveyard, sharing it with her lost son, in spirit at least. On that particular day she was reading from T S Eliot's Four Quartets: 'And the end of all our exploring will be to arrive where we started and know the place for the first time.'

A voice joined the one in her head reading the words, a dark chocolate-coloured voice from over her left shoulder. She half-turned. The man was smiling down at her. He said no more, just took her hand to help her up and led her to the wooden bench outside the north porch. Bunny, returned early from school with a nosebleed, saw them from his bedroom window. He saw them sit down, for he said as much to his mother later. He asked her who the man was and she replied merely that he was a stranger, a passing stranger. Bunny was touchy in those months, and she tried not to react when he cried out without warning about little things, though in truth she very often felt like crying out herself. She wanted to do that this time, asking what harm there was in kindness from a stranger, but she did not, for she knew how painful it was to the child that he had lost a brother and feared that in some as yet unfathomed way he was losing his father too.

This time we can call the man Stephen, for a name is simply a useful label and the Plankton Collector uses whichever label would be most appropriate in the circumstances. For Mary he had been Mr Smith. When he met Bunny – for this would happen, when the right time came – he would let the boy find the most fitting name. For Rose, Stephen was a comforting name. She had, she told him, had a schoolfriend of that name. Or rather, it was the brother of a school-friend. She laughed, surprised at herself for doing so, as she told him with blushing cheeks of how she had had a crush on the young man.

'We were only teenagers,' she said, realising as she did so that they were now sitting not in the churchyard but on a grassy cliff, and that her companion was unfastening the leather straps of a wicker picnic basket. She felt young again. She felt, in that moment, as if anything were possible, any problem could be overcome. A little way off two young people were playing with a dog, a black Labrador. Rose felt that she recognised them, but couldn't quite think from where. Stephen stood and called to them.

'Harriet, Tom, tea's ready!'

When they arrived, breathless, and flopped down with the panting dog, Stephen said:

'Look who I found Rose, on the same path as us! I asked them to join us for tea. You don't mind do you? There'll be plenty.'

There were cheese and pickle sandwiches and ham ones

with mustard and Rose's favourite, salmon and cucumber. And lashings of fresh lemonade. Tom tried to give a corner of his sandwich to the dog and she pulled out the whole slice of ham and ran off with it. Then the four young people lay down on the grassy sward and closed their eyes against the glare of the sun and one of them said this was going to be the very best of summers and it had to be because there was talk of a war coming and who knew where they would all be in a year's time.

They stayed till the shadows had crept over them and the sun had retreated to the horizon. Sitting up now, and close together looking out to sea, they spoke quietly of their plans. Tom was going to London to start his traineeship in his father's firm. Harriet, his sister, wanted to be an aeroplane pilot, or a mechanic.

'Or most anything,' she said, staring to the horizon with a determined face, 'that isn't stupidly girly. I want to do something really worthwhile.'

'Becoming a wife and mother was supposed to be worthwhile too,' Rose said to Stephen. She shivered, for the sun had left the churchyard, where they were once again sitting on the bench, close together as they had been with the two young people on the sea cliff. She turned to look at him, a silent pleading in her eyes. In her pocket her hand closed round some tiny shells she had picked up from the grass on the cliff top, dropped there by birds, no doubt.

'What do you think happened to those young people?' she asked.

'Killed in the war, both of them,' he said. 'Tom in an early bomb in the City; Harriet in a freak accident. It could have happened any time. She was damned unlucky. Cycling on a narrow road, a car turning into it in front of her, making her wobble and fall. She didn't stand a chance.' His voice tailed off.

After a while Stephen said he had to go, but hoped to see her again, perhaps in the same place one day. Rose watched him as he walked away. She wanted to call after him, but to say what, she didn't know. She did know she ought to be getting back home, but she stayed, alone on the bench, thinking about the people she had known before the war, and then of her friend Sally and their days in the flat in West Hampstead after that hateful fighting was all over and the world seemed fresh-minted. But it was an illusion. Sally had died and now her dear son Edgar was gone too. Nothing made sense, the friendships made and lost, the children born and raised, then.... She hated the word death, but it was at her heels the whole time.

She looked around the churchyard, at the graves, some neatly kept, others, the older ones, overgrown with ivy. And yet this was a place she came to seek peace. She shook her head, as if doing that would order her thoughts. Turning, she thought she saw Stephen over by the new grave where she had seen him first that afternoon, but when she blinked it seemed it had been no more than a trick of the light. Curious, she walked over to the new grave. She had a presentiment that she would see some warning on it, her own name perhaps or that of her husband, but no, it was an elderly woman from the village. She remembered now, the funeral had been the week before, she had seen the mourners from her garden, they had been very few.

As she walked back across the field between the churchyard and her own garden, Rose made a decision. A decision to talk properly to her husband. It was, she knew, no good putting all the blame on David, and certainly no good expecting him to come to her and explain himself. If she was to allow this gap between them, this fissure, to widen, a hole would open that would become a chasm into which the whole edifice that was their marriage and family would fall. But she got home to find Bunny and Mary both in tears, fretful that she too had left them for ever, and she had to put aside thoughts of preparing a meal of her husband's favourite foods and instead make the nursery food which her children craved when feeling sickly or sad. She boiled eggs, made toast into soldiers and spread them with Marmite. The three of them sat together at the kitchen table, the radio playing music quietly in the background, and planned a day out.

'Tomorrow,' she said. 'We'll go tomorrow. Never mind school. We'll see Daddy off to Town and we'll get the Down train straight after. We'll take egg and cress sandwiches and lemonade and at the seaside we'll paddle and then we'll picnic and then we'll collect shells.'

She realised that Mary's eyes were closing, and lifted her and carried her up to bed. The girl was asleep before they got to her bedroom. Downstairs, Bunny too was nearly asleep at the table. Rose looked at the clock. Eight thirty. David was still not home.

By the time her husband returned to the night-becalmed house, Rose was in bed and asleep herself, one arm flung above her head as if in resignation. In the morning he woke first and was up and shaving by the time she stirred. She stretched out her right arm to his side of the bed and was relieved to feel the residual warmth of his body. Then she remembered her promise to the children and jumped up guiltily, though she knew that in truth she was not the one who had any real reason to feel guilty.

After breakfast, the picnic hastily made, the family walked together to the station. On either side of the gravel path the hedges were filling out, the hawthorn leaves curling open. Rose laughed and said, 'If we'd been too late to make our picnic we could have gathered some of these leaves. Country people used to nibble them. They called them bread and cheese.'

Bunny and Mary wanted to taste the hawthorn, but pulled faces at the bitterness, and spat the leaves out onto the verge. Their father started to reprimand them but the whistle of the Up train sounded from the next station, and he put his hand on his hat and said he must run. Rose and the children watched him go, each one of them with a heavy heart and forlorn thoughts, but no-one was willing to speak of it.

'Come on,' said Rose, 'our train will be there in ten minutes. We're going to have a perfectly lovely day out.'

Each one of them made an effort, but the Plankton Collector, watching from a place where none of them could see him, knew that they were not happy. The children's running on the beach was not carefree; their mother would have appeared to the casual observer to be reading a book, but she was distracted and could not concentrate, reading one page over and over and finally putting the book aside and watching Bunny and Mary on the water's edge. At lunchtime sand got into the sandwiches and the lemonade spilt. Rose gathered up the children and they walked to a small café at the edge of the beach where she bought them ice-cream and, for herself, tea. The day was not lost, that much she said to herself. They had not been defeated by the bigger picture. And as they rode home on the train mother and daughter both fingered the shells which they kept in their pockets to remind them of the mysterious yet strangely familiar man they had met who they knew respectively as Stephen and Mr Smith. And each, independently, wondered if and when they would meet him again. They both fervently hoped they would do so, though neither of them would have been able to say why.

4

I'm twelve and I'm the middle child. I get Edgar's hand-me-downs. Correction, I used to get Edgar's hand-me-downs, before he went and died. My sister Mary gets special treatment because she's a girl, like Mother taking tea to her in the orchard in summer. Or she used to. Mother is distracted these days. I don't know where I fit in now. I wish Edgar was still here. There's stuff I need to talk about. Stuff I can't talk about with a stupid girl. I'm not sure whether I could talk to Father but he's never here anyway.

***

A few days after the seaside outing it started raining. It rained so much that a river started flowing though the garden of the house in the middle of England. Through the garden – from which the croquet hoops were taken up – and round the edge of the churchyard. Fields around were flooded, crops ruined and when the school holidays came, the children were confined to home by the rising waters. Bunny didn't mind the rain. When he woke in the morning and heard the gentle pitter-patter of raindrops on the window he wriggled his toes and snuggled down in his comfortable bed. He felt safe there. When Mother called him to hurry up and get dressed he didn't answer. When he eventually crept down the back stairs and into the kitchen he did it so quietly she wouldn't see him until a small noise made her turn from the stove where she was cooking lunch. Then she would frown but he would answer with an apologetic grin which he knew she couldn't resist and she would come over and ruffle his hair with a floury hand. Or rather, that was what Bunny hoped she would do. It was what she used to do to Edgar. Now that Edgar was gone he, Bunny, was the eldest child. That was what he told himself, but he couldn't make it real, either for himself or his mother. He was condemned to remain the middle child, the one who lost out both ways.

On the first of August, the rain stopped. What woke Bunny was the slam of the front door as Father left for work, but what kept him awake that morning was the total quiet that followed. There was no sound of rain on the window. The light had changed too. Bunny got up, dressed, made the briefest possible visit to the bathroom and almost fell down the stairs in his hurry to get out of the house. He drove his feet into his galoshes, because he knew the ground would be sodden, but, seeing the blue spreading across the sky, dared to leave his raincoat at home.

'Bunny, don't you want any breakfast?' Rose called after him.

He was already halfway down the garden and waved and shouted to his mother that he didn't need any. He had an apple and a bar of chocolate in his trouser pocket, to eat when he reached the den. He hadn't been there since Edgar had died, hadn't been able to even think of going there, but now it was as if something was pulling him towards it, almost against his will. When he reached the wooden lean-to he hesitated before pushing the door open. Inside, it took a few moments for his eyes to adjust. He had half-expected the old den to have been damaged, but apart from the damp it was as he remembered. He sat on one of the low seats they had made from Mother's old seed trays and pulled out his chocolate.

'Got a piece of that to spare?'

The voice startled Bunny and his reaction was to shove the chocolate back into his pocket as if guilty of some crime.

'Sorry to startle you, old chap.' It was a man dressed like

a gardener. 'I'm here to do a bit of tidying up, didn't your mother tell you?'

'No, but,' Bunny stopped, not really knowing what to say. His mother might well have asked someone to help in the garden, and as he'd rushed out so quickly she hadn't had a chance to tell him. He pulled the chocolate out of his pocket again and held it out to the stranger, who broke a piece off.

'Thanks. Mind if I sit down?'

Bunny wanted to say no, he wanted to be alone, but he just nodded and the man perched himself on Edgar's seat. They sat there together quietly chewing their chocolate and that seemed to help.

'Want to talk about it all, Bunny old man?' said the stranger.

Had he told him his name? Bunny didn't think so, nor did he remember the man telling him *his* name, but he found when he came to reply that he knew it.

'I do, Mr George, I do," he said.

'No need for the Mr, just call me George,' the man replied.

And Bunny found that he could talk about almost everything to George, about how he felt about being the middle child, about his brother dying and how his mother had seemed to go right down inside herself afterwards and nearly, very nearly, about his father, but not quite because he didn't have the words, they were just beyond his reach. The gardener listened and then they sat together in silence for a while longer.

'Must be getting back to work,' said George. 'Want to give me a hand?'

When Rose looked out of a first-floor window she saw the gardener and Bunny working together and smiled. At lunchtime she took them out sandwiches and lemonade and spread a rug. Mary ran down to join them. After they had eaten Rose lay back on the rug. She could smell the sea. With her eyes closed she was on the grassy cliff with Stephen that day in the spring. Then the scent of lavender took over and she was in her own garden again, but sitting up and looking sideways at the gardener she felt, more than saw, that he had something in common with that mysterious spring visitor.

'Do you know...?' she began, but stopped herself because it was preposterous.

But he seemed to understand because he smiled and nodded. Suddenly embarrassed, Rose jumped up and gathered up the picnic things.

'Come on children,' she said. 'We must let Mr George get on with the gardening.'

As he watched the woman and her children walking up the garden path, Mary skipping and Bunny trailing behind, the man who had told them his name was George put his hand into his left pocket, rattled a few shells which were in there and smiled to himself. Then he returned to his work.

The sun shone all afternoon and by six o'clock the gardener had finished work on the long herbaceous border. He straightened up to see Rose approaching. Without asking, he took her hand and led her to the bench outside the church. When they sat down she saw that this was Stephen.

'I have to attend to Edgar's grave,' she said.

He watched as she removed the old flowers, emptied the water, fetched fresh water and arranged flowers that she had picked from the border where he had been working – blue forget-me-nots and cornflowers with sprigs of frothy white gypsophila. Rose sat back on her heels and bowed her head for a few minutes and then returned to the bench. The man, whoever he be, Stephen or George, was gone. On the bench where he had been sitting was a scattering of small shells. She ran her fingers over them. They reminded her of something, someone, somewhere, just beyond recall. She picked them up and put them into her pocket, then walked back slowly to the house.

During the previous six weeks, the six weeks when it had rained every day, not one of those days had passed without Rose thinking about how she was going to broach with her husband the subject of his absences. She made and remade her resolution to talk with him. It was such a simple thing. She saw it clearly in her mind. The table laid for the two of them, once the children were in bed, or, better still, dispatched for the night to friends. Except that they seemed to find it so difficult to make friends. And that of course was part of what she needed to talk to David about. Such a simple thing, and she could not accomplish it. She needed help. Could this stranger be the one who could help her, she wondered. She laughed at herself for even thinking it, as he came and went without warning. Rose pushed the idea away but it kept returning to her mind, and she found herself looking for Stephen every day when she walked over to the churchyard. But August faded without her seeing him again. And at least three times a week David was not home by the time Rose went to bed.

5

I married Rose. I needed a wife. I told her that I had had a sister who had died young, but perhaps speaking in the way that I did was the wrong thing to do because she turned from me, so early on. I did not tell her any lies. But it is true that I did not tell her everything, how could she have understood? But I do my bit. I work hard and I give her money. And I have given her children. Three children. One of them died. It happens. We all have to find our own ways of coping.

***

David was a troubled man. He had been troubled for a long time, since the summer before Edgar had died. More troubled than he could admit or show to his wife or his children. The finances of the company were shaky and he needed to stay late at the office to work on the books. His secretary Janette was a great support and often stayed for a little too, though she had, he thought, an elderly mother who relied on her for meals so she couldn't be very late. She was apologetic about this, but David never put pressure on her, of that he was quite sure. So that when one evening she was still there at seven o'clock he expressed surprise that she was able to stay.

'It's no bother,' she said, holding his gaze rather longer than felt comfortable. 'I've nothing else to do.'

David found himself disturbed by his reaction to this. He wanted and did not want Janette to stay. He was not used to examining his emotions, and so did not at first understand what was happening, and that he was, in fact, physically attracted to the young woman. As they worked he found himself looking at the curve of her body and immediately blushing with embarrassment. It had never been like this with his own wife. He had never expected it to be so with any woman. With Rose he did his duty, or rather had done so by giving her the children. It had literally never occurred to him to continue to give her physical attention, and neither had his body stirred him in this way, till now. David lived his life mainly in his head. He knew what was right and what was wrong in the world of business. In which women were always secretaries; as wives at home were always mothers.

David had of course had a physical – he shied from the word sexual – encounter before he married Rose. His father had arranged it with a woman from another town. It had been shocking to him, and had almost put him off the whole idea of marriage. If he had been asked to describe it, David would have used words like brief and explosive. The thing that had happened was something not really connected to him. It was a rite of passage, that was the expression his father had used, a useful label to tie onto something so that it could be filed away. It did not need to be brought out again. Or if it was, it would be like a museum specimen, dulled with age and apparently innocuous.

What happened that evening in the small room at the back of the office happened without David thinking about it. It was clear, after the event, that it was a different matter for Janette, who had thought about it for weeks before, and had, David realised far too late, entrapped him. Like the rite of passage before marriage, it was brief and explosive, but less easily set aside, for Janette remained his secretary, sitting there demurely in front of him day after day, taking his instructions just as before. Except that things were not as they were before. She had ignited something long dormant within him, which thrilled and disgusted him in equal measure.

At home he allowed the disgust to predominate. If he was not to regard his secretary with lust, neither would he so regard his wife. If he could feign coldness there then maybe he could do the same with Janette. He was sadly mistaken. All he managed to do was cultivate an atmosphere of unhappiness at home and a state of unbearable tension in the office. There was a way to relieve the tension at work, of course, and he took that way, unable to see an alternative. Several times a week, once the junior staff had left, he would ask Janette to make tea and thereafter they enacted a ritual which they perfected over the weeks and months. Afterwards they continued with the work of the business. One thing upon which he insisted was that they should never kiss, for that was something which he reserved for his wife. And to him, kissing was a chaste act. Janette knew that he was married, in fact she liked to be reminded of that. It excited her.

David knew that the miserable affair had no future. He knew he should do something to extricate himself from it. But he was weak. He started going into the office on Sundays, even asking Janette in front of other staff if she could come in too. He wondered whether the only way out would be if someone discovered what was going on between them. He wanted, and yet of course he did not want, someone to do so.

Then Edgar fell ill. His wife was distraught. He should have been there, for her, for the boy. He knew that. He did the opposite. He did this even though he knew it would ruin him. Edgar died. His wife was inconsolable. His other children were bewildered. He could face none of them. He could no more talk to Rose than sprout wings and fly. All this time Janette obliged him. He stayed out with her more and more. He came home later and later. His mistress appeared to be physically insatiable. She told him that she was not looking for love and this was as well, for he had no love to give.

And one day, as suddenly as it had begun, it ended. Janette told him that her circumstances were such that she needed to leave promptly at five, every day. There would be no more coming into the office on a Sunday. There was clearly to be no discussion. David had no basis on which to argue. But he was left in a state of utter frustration, physically and mentally.

Returning home from the office after Janette had made her announcement, David found himself looking around for women on the train. Fortunately, there were none, only men of a certain age, as grey and tired-looking as himself. David shivered, afraid for what he might have been tempted to do, had he encountered a woman. Any woman, so deep was his degradation. Yet when he got home, where his wife was already in bed, he turned from her as if she were an inert object and went to the bathroom, where he attended to himself. It was, he knew, a pitiable state of affairs. His own heavy breathing meant that he was not aware of Rose approaching until he saw a shadow at the door. At his sharp intake of breath, she turned and fled. When he reached the bedroom, she was, apparently, already asleep and he dared not disturb her.

The following morning David woke, feeling, he said, pains in his arms and legs. Rose telephoned to his office and made an urgent appointment for him with a doctor, but within only two hours he seemed unable to walk, so the doctor called at the house after his morning surgery. After examining and talking with him, the doctor spoke with Rose.

'All in the mind,' he said, with what Rose thought was insensitive brusqueness. 'Has he suffered some kind of emotional trauma?'

Rose felt like saying that David's behaviour over the past weeks and months had caused the rest of family emotional trauma, but she knew that was not what the doctor wanted to hear, or to which he would be sympathetic.

'I know of nothing,' she replied.

The doctor grunted. 'Keep an eye on him. Call me if he deteriorates.' And was gone.

Rose found David sitting up in bed, reading a book and looking bright and to all intents and purposes normal.

'Are you still in pain?' she asked.

'I am,' he said. 'I will take my meals in bed.'

Rose turned away from her husband so that he would not see her expression. He settled to his reading, and when she brought him lunch she found him slumped asleep and felt, for a moment, guilty. Perhaps, she thought, he really had been over-doing it at work and quite simply needed rest. And that was what she told the children. They should not disturb their father, she said, and should play quietly away from the house.

The Plankton Collector was, of course, aware of all that had happened, including the episodes of which David was so ashamed. He did not pass judgement, that was not his job, but he noted everything and considered how best he could help. It was, he felt, not yet time to approach David. He genuinely did need to rest before he would be able to even consider any change in his behaviour. Rose's mind and spirit were busy with the needs of her husband. He decided to let them settle together in the house. They could do this best without the children, of course. So his task was to occupy them. There were only a few days of their summer holidays remaining, and, with the weather set fair, it was time for a long-lost uncle to appear. A rich uncle who could come along and whisk Bunny and Mary away on holiday.

It was Bunny who picked up from the doormat the post-card from Uncle Barnaby announcing his imminent arrival.

'Who is he, Mother?' he asked, jumping up and down with excitement. 'You have never told us about this uncle.'

In truth, Rose had herself forgotten that she had such a brother, though later she thought it ridiculous that anyone could forget such a close relative, particularly a rich one, however long the interval since they had met. When Barnaby arrived, of course, she knew him, as she had known Stephen and George, through some sense beyond the normal five, something which she described to herself, when she thought about it, as fundamental, and she had no doubt that she could trust him to look after her children.

6

Uncle Barnaby had arrived the very next day, travel in those now-distant days being largely unproblematic, if apparently slower, and so actually often faster. That was one of the lessons which he taught Mary and Bunny on their journey to the island. They took the Down train to the coast, a bus to the little port, a boat and then, when they reached the island, a cart drawn by a tractor which took them to a small white-washed cottage with roses on the wall and a garden which opened onto a sandy beach in a horseshoe-shaped bay. They arrived in time for tea, which was already laid out for them on a white table-cloth in the kitchen. They were to stay there for a whole week.

That week felt to both children as if it were the whole summer. They forgot the rain that had fallen for six weeks at home, they forgot the awkwardnesses and unhappinesses of the big house now so far away in the middle of England where they lived, and settled into the small comfortable spaces of the whitewashed house on the island. They saw no-one and missed no-one. What they had was enough. How food appeared on the table they did not know, nor did they ask. What they had was simple but plentiful. Uncle Barnaby built sandcastles with them and all three swam in the calm warm water as if it was their element. Indeed, there were days when her supposed uncle appeared to Mary to be more like a dolphin, but Bunny said she was a dopey girl and had too much imagination. Uncle Barnaby told them both, as they sat out in the dusk that day, watching the fireflies in the hedges that bordered the garden, that imagination was a wonderful thing. You could never have too much of it.

'Look,' he said. 'You can imagine that those fireflies are fairies, casting a spell on us so that we have good dreams.'

He told them too that imagination was what would save them.

'It is what will save all of us,' he said. 'Otherwise the dull ones will pull us all down into misery.'

'Is that what has happened to Father?' asked Bunny, able at last, in this place of refuge, to ask.

But Uncle Barnaby tousled the boy's hair in a way that felt strangely familiar and said he was not to worry about his father, they were there for a holiday and it would do everyone good, their mother and father included.

'Let's go onto the beach,' he said, jumping up. 'I've got

something to show you both.'

As soon as they walked through the garden gate, all three of them stopped stock-still. It was by this time nearly dark, and out to sea the water appeared almost black, but where it ran onto the beach there was a wide strip that was a brilliant and beautiful blue.

'That colour is made by tiny creatures,' said Uncle Barnaby, and when they were back in the cottage he made hot chocolate for the children and told them the story of the plankton which they had seen glowing in the dark. Although the beach appeared at first sight to be sandy, he said, it was actually made up of millions of very tiny shells. Each of the shells had been home to an incredibly small creature, like the ones that had made the beach-light. When they died, as every living thing will do, he said, their shells sank to the bottom of the sea and were, in time, washed up on the shore. They were like memories of the creatures which had lived in them, he said.

'You can collect those you like best and make pictures from them,' he told the children.

The next morning, Mary and Bunny were down on the beach early. At breakfast-time they returned with a bucketful of shells. At first sight the shells all looked the same, but Uncle Barnaby produced a microscope, and when they looked at them through this they saw all sorts of different shapes, oblongs, diamonds and stars, twinkling with the many blues and greens of the sea. They cleared a big space on the floor of the cottage and the children started to arrange them into a wheeling, whirling picture, which grew in size and complexity by the day as they collected more shells and learned how to differentiate between them.

As they worked on the picture, they talked about their own memories, and especially about their lost brother. They found on the following days that as they played upon the beach it was as if Edgar were with them, just out of sight but about to return.

When the day came for them to leave, the children wanted to take the shell picture with them. But Uncle Barnaby said that this was not possible.

'Not now,' he said. 'Not just now, but you will remember it.'

'You will remember this place,' he continued, 'and you will always be able to come back to it in your minds. No-one can take your happy memories away from you.'

And, not understanding, for they had not lived long enough to feel the weight of memory, Mary and Bunny wept. They continued to do so all the way home, bemoaning that they had ever come away, and when Uncle Barnaby delivered them back to their parents, the children did not even thank him for taking them away on holiday. But the Plankton Collector was not upset. In his line of work nothing surprised him and he knew that no-one in the family was yet able to see the complete picture.

He, Barnaby, Rose's long-lost brother as he was at this time, stayed for a while and talked with his sister and her husband after the children had gone to bed. He told them about the island and the bay, a place of which they had apparently never heard. They didn't even seem to be familiar with its name, but again this did not surprise him. He gave them the directions so that one day they might go there again as a family. Then, as it was late and the last trains would have left, Rose said she would make up a bed for her brother. He said he would like to sleep in Edgar's old room, which made her hesitate. She had not been in the room since she had stripped the bedding after her son's death.

'Give me the sheets,' said the visitor. 'I can make up the bed.'

In the room, the air was colder than elsewhere in the house, in spite of all the windows having been kept shut for more than half a year. Barnaby opened a window to let in the last of the heat of the day, and there followed a mingling of what was lost and what was still to be. He slept soundly. He had no qualms about the boy having died in the room. He knew better than most about the cycle of life.

Downstairs in the kitchen, Rose and her husband were still up. During the week their children had been away with Barnaby the two of them had begun a rapprochement. Each day David had rested, he had felt a little stronger. Each day after she had visited her elder son in the churchyard, Rose prepared the evening meal, simple food cooked with love. Each day they sat and ate together. On the first days they did not speak much, it was enough to be in one another's company. It was, as it were, a fresh courting. Then, on the third day, David told his wife of his infidelities. It was what she had feared and it was to her like a physical wounding.

'You have broken my heart'" she said starkly, for it was so.

And yet it was more complicated than this, for Rose knew that she was not herself without blame. She had withdrawn from David, and worse, she had thought of others, even though she had never done anything, certainly never made a move towards anyone else. All this she confessed to him on the fourth day. For him it was a kind of relief, a sharing of the burden of guilt. So that from that day there was a turning in their relationship, the smallest, microscopic degree of change of an angle, a movement towards one another that was almost imperceptible at first, but palpable to both of them.

On the following day, they walked through the garden together. David noticed, perhaps for the first time, what wonders his wife had done there, and praised her for the glory of the flower borders. In the orchard, he dared to take Rose's hand. She allowed this but kept her eyes cast down. Then, gradually, she returned the slight pressure of fingers entwining with fingers, a small but significant sign of returning affection and trust. After lunch, they sat quietly together reading. From time to time, they would look up from their books, exchanging tentative smiles which became stronger as the afternoon wore on.

On the sixth day, the morning sky was a burgeoning blue, with just high wisps of cloud. A fair-weather sky, thought David, looking at it from the breathless calm of the orchard where it was so quiet he could hear wasps sucking on the juice of the bursting plums.

'What shall we do with this day?' he asked his wife over breakfast. 'It may be the last day of summer, and it is entirely ours.'

They packed bread, cheese, tomatoes and fruit from the garden, and they walked out, across the fields, pausing now and then to look at brown butterflies on a beech hedge or a passing hawker dragonfly which was hovering and examining them too. When they reached the river, they spread a rug and sat like the young lovers they had once been, content now to share the silence of the day. Or rather to listen to all the sounds of nature which emerge when the noises made by humans subside – the buzzings of bees, tiny whirrings of insect wings, the bubbling of a stream and the whisper of the summer breeze. Something made Rose turn to her left, and for a moment she saw, or thought she saw, a man walking towards them, raising an arm in greeting. Stephen, George, Barnaby, which of them was it, she wondered. But then he was gone and she thought it a trick of the light through the trees, or something from her imagination. She turned back to her husband and smiled.

'This is a truly lovely day,' she said.

'Yes it is,' he agreed, and truly meant it.

And so it was that they readied themselves for Barnaby to return with their children the following day. They were, separately and together, pleased to see them, and said as much to one another when all three of the travellers were in bed and just the two of them left sitting in the night kitchen mulling over the events of the week, sharing thoughts as they vowed they would continue to do from then on.

7

After Uncle Barnaby's trip to the island with Mary and Bunny, the Plankton Collector thought that his work was nearly done. But, remarkable as he was, he was not omniscient or omnipotent and there was a set-back to come, as has happened time and again in the history of our Earth.

It was September. Edgar had been dead for nine months, and Rose no longer felt the need to visit his grave every single day, but knew him to be with her as the other children were, albeit in an altered way. It troubled her, though, that her husband never spoke of the boy, and that was a splinter in their relationship, something which remained below the surface and could suddenly produce a sharp pain if any pressure was applied to a particular spot. This is what happened one day, on one ordinary day in the autumn. It was a Sunday, the whole family around the lunch table. Rose had roasted a joint of beef for a treat.

'Edgar always said Granny's gravy was best,' said Mary, from nowhere.

'Never mind Edgar,' he father replied, his voice higher than usual. 'He's not here any more. Don't be so impolite to your mother.'

Rose burst into tears, Bunny scampered from the room, knocking over the gravy boat in his haste to get up from the table, David tried to mop up the gravy which was dripping onto the red tiles of the kitchen floor and Mary looked on bemused. Her father snarled at her:

'Go to your room.'

She went. Silence fell between her parents.

'So still he comes between us all,' said Rose quietly when she had stopped crying.

'What are we to do?' She raised her eyes to her husband but he lowered his head.

'I have tried, David,' she cried out. 'I have tried my hardest.'

'And you know that I have tried too,' he said. 'But it is never enough, it seems.'

The two of them sat in awkward silence.

'Often,' she said after some minutes, 'I feel as if I am living behind a sheet of glass. You see me but you do not hear me. And I am powerless to break the glass.'

'And you think *I* can break it?' he asked.

'No, I don't.' Her voice broke as she said the bleak words.

'We have to try together, then, Rose,' said David. 'For all our sakes.'

Their conversation coiled on through the afternoon, stopping and starting, getting tangled in misunderstandings which they pulled tight in exasperation and then had to patiently unpick. They cleared the half-eaten lunch things together, and at tea-time called the children, for all four of them were hungry, whether or not they were prepared to admit it. After tea, David said he was going out, he needed to clear his head. Rose watched as he walked down the garden, through the gate into the churchyard and stopped at Edgar's grave. What she did not see, for he kept himself in the shadows, was the man who joined her husband there.

'He is at peace,' said the voice from behind David. 'That grave contains his bones, that is all. He is not there, yet he is everywhere.'

David turned. The man was a stranger to him, yet strangely familiar.

'Have we met before?' he asked.

'Ah,' said the man. 'We have all met everyone else before, but we do not always remember when and where. We pass one another on the street years before we are introduced. We meet our future loves at bus stops or stand next to them on railway station platforms and know them not.'

David felt impatient with this elliptical talk, but remained polite.

'Ah,' he replied. 'It may be so. Are you visiting the area?'

'Indeed, indeed,' replied the man. 'But I fear I have strayed from my way. Can you perhaps help me?'

David jumped to his feet, glad of something practical to distract him from his own and the visitor's philosophical musings.

The man introduced himself as Colin. The mention of the name had a visceral effect on David. He swallowed down his feeling, which was of a nostalgia so deep as to be bottomless, and led the man from the churchyard. Once they were on the path which led towards the railway station the man seemed to take charge, without making it at all obvious, and began to lead David, rather than the other way round. At the very moment they arrived on the railway platform, the Down train arrived and, as if they had planned it, more than that, as if they had planned it as a pair of long-lost chums, they jumped aboard eagerly.

It was now early morning. It did not occur to David to

wonder what had happened to the intervening evening and night, or whether Rose would worry, or indeed, it being Monday, whether he would be missed at the office. None of these things occurred to him because he was, once again, seventeen years old, and going on an adventure with his friend Colin. So easily are some of the mysteries of life solved. The train journey was long but they passed the time by playing card games. A small ginger kitten appeared on the luggage rack, and they realised that it must have been forgotten by a previous passenger. Colin said he would find the guard and left the kitten in David's care while he went in search of the man.

David stroked the kitten, which climbed onto his shoulder. Its loud purring sent David into a deep slumber and when he awoke it was dark. The kitten was gone and it was Colin's tousled head which rested on David's shoulder, his breath like a soft purr in his friend's ear. The train was passing along the edge of the sea. David could make out the shapes of palm trees. Then sleep reclaimed him until the warmth of the morning sun on his cheek caused him to stir once more.

When the two of them got off the train they were ravenously hungry. Down the street of the small Italian town at which they had disembarked, they found a restaurant where an elderly lady dressed in black served them eggs and ham with crusty bread, a flagon of wine and a wry smile. Then she showed them a room with an iron bedstead, a horsehair mattress and a sink in the corner. They both knew they had found a paradise, a paradise for one short week and one which would remain for ever their secret. Each day they went to the beach and swam. They gathered treasures from the beach to share with one another over the suppers which the lady in black prepared for them, clucking over them like a mother hen. There were myriad star-shaped shells, some quite large but most tiny. One evening, David spread them on the table and started making swirling patterns.

'I want to take them home,' said Colin, starting to gather them, but David put a hand on his friend's arm to stop him.

'We can take home only our memories,' he said. 'And you must swear to me that you will tell no-one of this.'

The two of them bowed their heads and shared a solemn promise. They would both return to England, marry as was expected of them, raise families and live happily ever after. Or, at the least, they would put on the very best show ever of doing so. Which was what David did.

Outside the churchyard, on that September Sunday afternoon, David watched the man who had said his name was Colin walking down the path towards the railway station. If he hurried, he had told him, he would just catch the Down train at a quarter past four. He saw Colin arrive at the station just as the train drew in, puffing smoke. He waved, and the man waved back with a yellow handkerchief, spotted with a darker colour. From a distance, David could not make out whether the spots were blue or black, but he found that he knew. Back then, when they were seventeen, Colin, the boy whom he had loved, had had a blue-spotted yellow handkerchief.

David sat down there at the roadside and he wept. He wept for Colin, killed, like so many, so many, in that despicable war which had bisected their lives. He wept for his wife, for the way in which he had deceived her on their honeymoon by talk of a sister who had died young, when it was Colin for whom he had mourned. He wept for Edgar, born into what was supposed to be a safe world and torn from it by a random illness. And, finally, he wept for himself. And his tears began to wash away the weight he no longer needed to carry within him.

8

The Plankton Collector had, now, completed his work with David. Of this he was confident. He realised that, in the guise of a man, he could not achieve the same with Rose. But he was of course able to act in other ways.

Rose did not know precisely what had happened on the afternoon her husband walked down to the churchyard after the unfinished Sunday lunch and the awkward convolutions of their conversation. What was clear, was that when he returned he had reached some kind of resolution. For her, that was enough. She did not need to question David further. In the following weeks, the weather matched their moods with an Indian summer of exquisite warmth and delicacy. The garden was full of red and golden tones. Rose cut late blooms from the herbaceous border and filled bowls throughout the house. By early October, the apple trees in the orchard were bowing down with the weight of the fruit. George came to help pick them, to the delight of Bunny, who climbed onto the man's strong shoulders to pick from the highest boughs. It seemed to Rose, looking on, that as they were relieved of their fruit the trees seemed almost to shake themselves upright again.

'I always think it's strange when people find the autumn a time of sadness,' George said to her as they stood side by side watching the children cartwheeling between the unburdened trees. 'To me it is a season of renewal.'

'I hope you're right,' she said. They said no more to one another, but Rose knew that there were still things unsaid, things that she needed to say to someone. But who?

The answer came with a telephone call from a woman who said she worked in some sort of Archives Office and had come across something which she thought would be of interest to her.

'Oh,' said Rose, uncertain of an appropriate response. 'What sort of thing?' she asked.

'Just records, family records, something you may not know' was all the woman would say.

They arranged to meet the following Monday, in town. Rose went to town so rarely she decided to make a day of it. She had never been one for shopping; living in the country she didn't need fancy clothes, so she would go instead to Regent's Park, walk in the rose garden and maybe even feed the ducks as she used to do with Sally, in that distant happy time.

'I'll go to the park where we first meet,' she said gaily to David. He did not need to know that her best memory was not of that time. There are, for each of us, memories we can keep to ourselves, things which we could use to hurt another, and which we can choose not to use in that way. That was something now understood between David and Rose.

In the park the leaves were turning, blowing, falling. Summer seemed long gone. Rose remembered what George had said about autumn being a time of renewal but she did not feel it so. Her steps were heavy. There were, though, still some roses in bloom, and she bent to inhale the scent of one which had an apricot blush. The perfume took her, took her back, and it was as if Sally were sitting beside her, as if it were that precious time before anything was fixed. Before anything was weighty or troubling. But Sally was not there. Sally was dead. Why had she thought that coming to this place would bring her back? Nothing brings back the past.

'Nothing brings back the past, you're right.' Rose turned to see who was apparently reading her thoughts, but there was no-one else sitting on the bench or standing anywhere near. Only an old dog, sitting on the ground and reaching out a paw.

'You think so too, old thing, do you?' It seemed the most natural thing in the world to talk to the dog. Rose found that saying all the things that were usually stuck inside her head was a great relief. After a while she got up and the dog padded alongside her as she walked through the gardens. When they reached the café, one of the staff gave her a bowl of water and a biscuit for the dog and they sat and took their refreshment together. Then they went their separate ways.

When Rose arrived at the address she had been given for the Archives Office she found it was a library. There was nobody there by the name the woman had given her on the telephone. She was mystified but in a way relieved. She had not wanted to be told of some distant relative who had died, which was what she had imagined. She had had enough of death. It was time to get on with life.

The Plankton Collector was visiting the churchyard when Rose arrived home on the train. He saw her walking back to the house, obviously eager to get home. She clearly had no further need of his services that day. Content with his afternoon's work, he moved on.

9

The second of November would have been Edgar's sixteenth birthday. Rose was determined that the day should not bring them down into sadness and remorse. There had already been enough of that for all of them. She had planned a tea party and made a special chocolate cake, one which was a family favourite, requested always by the children for their birthdays. David came home early from the office and they toasted teacakes on the fire in the parlour and told happy stories.

The ring at the doorbell surprised them all. Rose frowned and jumped up.

'I do hope it's not strangers who've lost their way,' she said, knowing that if it were so, she would have to invite them in.

David and the children heard her exclamation as she opened the front door, and they turned away from the fire to see.

Round the door there appeared the little ginger head of a kitten, followed by the much larger head of Uncle Barnaby. And from his pocket he drew a second kitten, ginger like his brother.

'Presents!' he exclaimed. 'For you,' he continued, handing one to Mary and the other to Bunny.

The room filled with squeals of delight, from the children and from the kittens. And their parents and Uncle Barnaby looked on with wide smiles.

The party continued into the evening. Rose had invited the neighbours for drinks. Everyone seemed to congregate in the kitchen as they do on such occasions. Over the heads, David fancied that he saw Colin. At one point Rose, moving through with a tray of little savoury pastries, had a fleeting glimpse of Stephen. As for Uncle Barnaby, he was upstairs reading bedtime stories to the children, though when their mother put her head around their bedroom doors Bunny and Mary were both sound asleep and there was no sign of Barnaby. In the parlour, the kittens were curled up together in a basket in front of the guarded embers of the fire.

The next morning, Mary crept downstairs early to play with the kittens, so she was the first to see the other present which Uncle Barnaby had brought them. At least she assumed it was him, for who else knew about the shell picture which they had begun to make during their week on the island that summer?

Hung on the wall was the completed picture, complex whorls of minute shells, reflecting and refracting the light into all the colours of the rainbow. Then, in turn, Bunny and their mother and father joined her in front of the picture. And although none of them knew how he had made it, or exactly how their separate bits of the bigger picture fitted together, they all somehow knew that this was a gift to them, to them as a family, from the man whom they had variously known as Stephen, Mr Smith, George, Uncle Barnaby and Colin. The man who was, in fact, the Plankton Collector. Who had enabled them to face their regrets and fears. Taught them the difference between the weight of unhappy memories and the lightness borne by happiness recalled. Had shown them how to live as a family once more. The man who had left them now and travelled on. Though he would be there, visible from the corner of an eye, whenever any one of them needed reassurance. For that is what we all need, now and then, on this journey we are taking, this journey through our life on Earth.

Cath Barton was born in the English Midlands and now lives in Abergavenny, south Wales. Her short stories have been published in anthologies in Australia, the US and the UK, most recently in *Normal Deviation* (Wonderbox Publishing) and *Nothing Is As It Was* (Retreat West Books) and in literary magazines *The Lonely Crowd* and *Strix*. She is also active in the online flash fiction community. Cath was Literature Edtor of California-based *Celtic Family Magazine* (2013–2016). She was awarded a place on the 2018 enhanced mentoring scheme for writers run by Literature Wales, working on a collection of short stories inspired by the work of the sixteenth-century Dutch artist Hieronymus Bosch.

Acknowledgements and Thanks

Thanks to and in memory of Francis Doherty (1932–1993), who as my English tutor at Keele University was the first to encourage me to write creatively. My early work was embarrassingly bad, but he was the kindest of teachers.

Thanks also to: Barry Chantler, who threw down the challenge to write a novella in the first place, when I was least expecting it. Fellow writers and members of The Word Counts in Abergavenny: Shirley Shirley, Goff Bradshaw, Jackie Bradshaw and June Penhelog, for being on the journey with me. Gwen Davies, Julia Forster and Bronwen Williams at New Welsh Review, for all their help and unfailing patience.

And, more than I can ever say, Oliver Barton, for everything.

Praise for *The Plankton Collector*

'Haunts like memory, shimmering in and out of love and loss with unexpected, poignant hope. Richly lyrical, beautifully original.'
  Helen Sedgwick, author of *The Growing Season*

'A brilliantly evoked examination of memory and innocence… delivers a kaleidoscope of compelling voices united by a spectral visitor, not from the heights, but the apparent depths. Haunting.'
  James Clammer, author of *Why I Went Back*

'Cath Barton tells the story… with a lyrical voice that is very much her own. This beautifully structured novella leads the reader to a resolution that is both moving and deeply satisfying.'
  Francesca Rhydderch, author of *The Rice Paper Diaries*

'Painterly… lush dreamy prose creates a vivid landscape, while its lyricism transports the reader. Cleverly creates a universe of new realities.'
  Cathryn Summerhayes

'A beautifully controlled mix of magical realism and nature writing about time, healing, trauma and the fluid, unreliable nature of memory.'
  David Lloyd, co-judge of the New Welsh Writing Awards 2017

WINNER OF THE NEW WELSH WRITING AWARDS 2016

Out now in print & ebook formats

'Triumphs, in its lean prose and true dialogue... disarming humour & evocation of a family divided by sexism & racism. Stitches together threads of memory to create a moving tapestry of lost life, building bridges of understanding across time and place, enhancing literature's ever-changing, ever-supple genre'

Rory MacLean

'Mandy Sutter's Nigeria rises like a mirage [creating] a complete arc of innovative concision'

New Welsh Review

'Atmospheric wonderfully unexpected disquieting, touching and darkly humorous'

Alison Moore

'We discern, in a microcosm, what has happened and is happening in macrocosm in much of the developing world'

Penelope Shuttle

WALES BOOK OF THE YEAR 2016 SHORTLIST
Out now in ebook format

'Quite beautiful. [The author encounters a culture that is
completely alien] and she does it with a poet's eye... precisely and
vitally. She reads this unfamiliarity with all her imaginative nerve-
endings open: the effect is quite remarkable... [reminiscent of] a
netsuke [in its] precision.'

Prof Tony Brown (WBOY adjudication)

Lightning Source UK Ltd.
Milton Keynes UK
UKHW042007090719
345865UK00001B/72/P

9 781916 150126